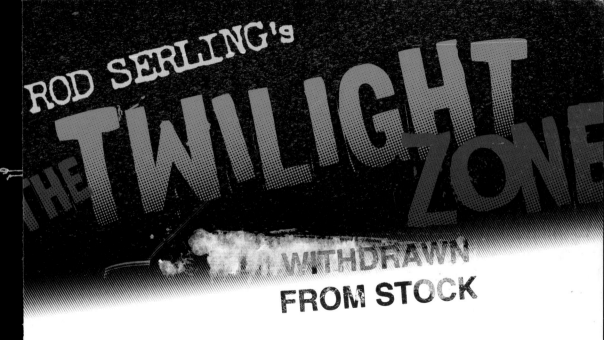

ROD SERLING's THE TWILIGHT ZONE

THE ODYSSEY OF FLIGHT 33

Adaptation from Rod Serling's original script by

MARK KNEECE

Illustrated by

ROBERT GRABE

BLOOMSBURY

LONDON BERLIN NEW YORK

INTRODUCTION

There is a fifth dimension beyond that which is known to man. It is a dimension as vast as space and timeless as infinity. It is the middle ground between light and shadow, between science and superstition, and it lies between the pit of man's fears and the summit of his knowledge. This is the dimension of imagination. It is an area which we call the Twilight Zone.

America, between the 1950s and early 1960s, was itself in a sort of "twilight zone." Following the victories of World War II and the attending economic boom—but before the Civil Rights marches; the assassinations of John F. Kennedy, Martin Luther King, Jr., and Robert F. Kennedy; and the Vietnam War—we were wrapped in a gleaming package of shining chrome, white picket fences, and Hollywood glamour. But beneath this shimmering facade lay a turbulent core of racial inequality, sexual inequality, and the Cold War threat of nuclear attacks from the Soviet Union. We'd never been more affluent—or more frightened.

Enter Rodman Edward Serling of Binghamton, New York. Serling began writing in his teens for his high school newspaper; as a student at Antioch College, he was already selling scripts to radio programs. While serving as a paratrooper in the U.S. Army Eleventh Airborne (for which he earned a Purple Heart), he wrote for the Armed Services Radio. He went on to write for film and television, first in feature presentations for *Hallmark Hall of Fame* and *Playhouse 90*, including the lauded "Requiem for a Heavyweight," perhaps drawing inspiration from his own experiences as a Golden Gloves boxer. More than two hundred of his teleplays were produced. In all, his work would win not only the adoration of listeners and viewers but a host of prestigious awards, including a record-breaking six Emmy awards—two of them for his greatest achievement, *The Twilight Zone*.

The worlds and characters presented over the course of five seasons, beginning in October 1959, were like nothing audiences had seen before. Television, the new "must have" appliance for America's increasingly prosperous households, offered comedies such as *I Love Lucy* and *The Honeymooners*, news programs including Edward R. Murrow's *See It Now*, as well as Westerns, game shows, and soap operas. With a typewriter as his spade, Serling dug beneath the surface of the expected and planted the seeds of a more imaginative and thoughtful genre, writing more than half of the show's 156 episodes while producing and hosting all of them. He bravely took on themes of oppression, prejudice, and paranoia, all the while giving people what they needed at the end of the day: entertainment.

While he had his run-ins with censorship, Serling's clever use of other worlds and veiled scenarios generally protected him. As he explained, what he couldn't have a Republican or a Democrat espouse on the show, he could have an alien profess without offending the sponsors. This approach also allowed viewers to take away whatever message best suited them; the more reflective could consider the psychological and political implications, while others might be satisfied with simply enjoying the thrill of the surface story. So much more than mere science fiction or fantasy, Serling's scripts are parables that explore the multifaceted natures of hope, fear, humanity, loneliness, and self-delusion.

Half a century later, *The Twilight Zone* remains a part of our culture, routinely referenced in print and on television, having become a shorthand expression that succinctly describes the bizarre and unexpected. The original episodes are still aired on the SciFi Channel, both in late-night slots and as day-long marathons. The show was literally a Who's Who of Hollywood, helping to foster the careers of fledgling actors including Robert Redford, Ron Howard, Dennis Hopper, Charles Bronson, and William Shatner. It has also inspired countless authors and filmmakers, who have gone on to break through boundaries of their own.

In the fifty years since *The Twilight Zone* first aired, we've faced new enemies and have altered our definitions of happiness, but our core hopes and fears remain the same, as does our desire to be entertained. The stories are as compelling, and as telling, as ever. And now, in their newest incarnation, Serling's scripts serve as the basis for this graphic novel series, which honors the original text and even echoes the storyboarding of television, but offers a fresh interpretation, as seen through the eyes of a new generation of artists.

—Anna Marlis Burgard
Director of Industry Partnerships, Savannah College of Art and Design

You're traveling through
another dimension,
a dimension not only of sight and sound
but of mind;
a journey into a wondrous land
whose boundaries

are that of imagination.

That's the signpost up ahead—

your next stop,

the Twilight Zone!

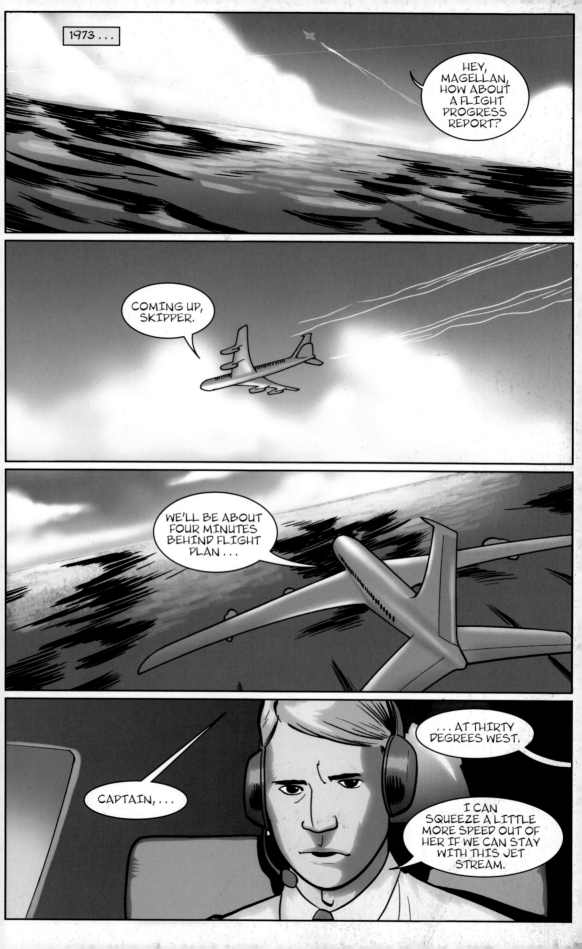

. . . GANDER WANTS TO KNOW IF YOU INTEND AN ALTITUDE CHANGE AFTER WE PASS THIRTY WEST.

ADVISE GANDER NEGATIVE. WE'RE GETTING A VERY NICE RIDE WHERE WE ARE.

GENTLEMEN, YOU'LL BE PLEASED TO KNOW THAT THANKS TO THE QUALITY OF THIS AIRCRAFT, THE FINE WEATHER, AND MY BRILLIANT FLYING . . .

WE'LL HIT JFK ON SCHEDULE IF OUR SPEED HOLDS UP.

SHANWICK, SHANWICK, COPY GANDER . . . TRANS-OCEAN FLIGHT 3-3 . . .

. . . POSITION: FIFTY NORTH, THIRTY WEST . . . FLIGHT LEVEL THREE-FIVE-ZERO.

SHANWICK RECEIVED, SKIPPER.

I LOVE LOOKING OUT AT THE CLOUDS AND THINGS.

LOOKS LIKE A—

PATCHWORK QUILT?

NAW. WE'RE OVER THE OCEAN. MORE LIKE A BIG MIRROR.

MIRROR, HUH?

UH-HUH.

I READ SOMEPLACE THAT SITTING ON PLANES FOR LONG PERIODS OF TIME CAUSES BLOOD CLOTS.

YOU GONNA HAVE TO EXCUSE ME A MINUTE. I ALREADY GOT SOME BAD VARICOSE VEINS.

YOU KNOW, WE'LL JUST HAVE TO DO THIS ALL OVER AGAIN WHEN I COME BACK. . . .

AND, YOUNG MAN, IF YOU DON'T MIND, PLEASE KEEP AN EYE ON MY PURSE— I HATE TO CARRY IT AROUND ALL THE TIME.

NAME'S DAWSON PINKNEY. I'M JUST ON MY WAY BACK FROM AN EXHIBITION OVER IN LONDON.

I PARACHUTED DOWN INTO THE BUCKINGHAM PALACE, SEE!

EVERYTHING OKAY, SKIPPER?

FINE. TRIM TABS NEED FINESSING FOR SOME REASON. AIR MUST BE A LITTLE UNSTABLE—CLEAR AS A BELL OUT THERE, THOUGH.

YOU FELLAS WANT SOME COFFEE?

THAT'S A BIG AFFIRMATIVE, MA'AM.

HOW WE DOIN' BACK THERE, JANIE?

YOUR FLIGHT ATTENDANTS WOULD LIKE TO GET TO NEW YORK A-S-A-P.

THE PASSENGERS, HOWEVER, ARE HIGHLY CONTENT—EXCEPT FOR ONE NUT JOB WHO WANTED PAULA TO PROVIDE HERBAL TEA.

SOME KIND OF STRESS CASE, I BET.

HERBAL TEA, HUH? HA. THERE'S ALWAYS ONE.

WOOO . . . THAT WAS FUNNY. LIKE DRIVING DOWNHILL TOO FAST . . .

I FELT IT TOO. A SENSATION OF ACCELERATION.

THAT'S WHAT I FELT.

ODD . . .

TRUE AIRSPEED 540. WE'RE LEVEL. S'POSE WE PICKED UP A TAILWIND?

MAYBE I'M JUST GETTING OLD.

WELL, I FELT IT. I GUESS I'M GETTING OLD TOO, HUH? GOOD-BYE, GENTLEMEN!

AWFULLY TOUCHY, ISN'T SHE?

HEH.

YOU CAN'T FEEL A TAILWIND. AND I STILL FEEL SOMETHING.

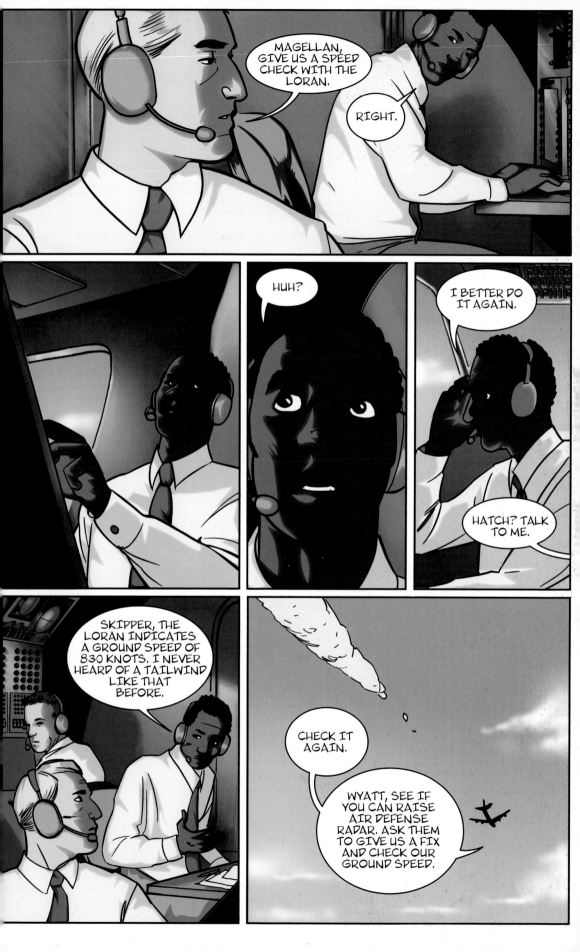

MAGELLAN, YOU SURE ABOUT THAT LORAN?

SKIPPER, IT'S DEAD ON . . . AND WE'RE STILL ACCELERATING. 980 . . .

1,120 . . .

1,500 . . .

GOD IN HEAVEN, I CAN'T EVEN KEEP UP WITH IT!

WYATT, ANYTHING FROM AIR DEFENSE RADAR?

2,100 . . .

NO, SIR, I CAN'T RAISE THEM.

I HOPE THE WINGS STAY ON.

THIS AIRPLANE IS HEADING INTO AN UNCHARTED REGION, WELL OFF THE BEATEN TRACK OF COMMERCIAL TRAVELERS.

IT'S MOVING INTO *THE TWILIGHT ZONE!* WHAT YOU'RE ABOUT TO SEE . . . WE CALL *"THE ODYSSEY OF FLIGHT 33."*

THINK YOU CAN PROD THE FLY PEOPLE AGAIN? I'M SEEING THE *RIDE OF THE VALKYRIES* TONIGHT.

WE'LL SEE. . . .

DID YOU CHECK IT AGAIN, MAGELLAN?

I'VE GOT . . .

STILL GOING FASTER—OFF THE SCALE . . . I'D SAY FIVE THOUSAND KNOTS AT THIS POINT.

THIS ISN'T MAKING ANY SENSE. STILL NOTHING, WYATT?

NOTHING, SKIPPER.

. . . COFFEE.

JANIE . . . I'VE ALWAYS HAD A THING ABOUT VALHALLA—AND GEORGE COLE, THE GUY WHO'S TAKING ME.

JANIE?

I HOPE THE VALHALLA YOU'RE TALKING ABOUT IS AT LINCOLN CENTER ON 65TH STREET IN LOVELY NEW YORK CITY.

INSTEAD OF?

INSTEAD OF THE REAL THING.

WE'RE IN TROUBLE.

HOW BAD?

I DON'T THINK THEY KNOW YET . . . BUT IT'S NOT GOOD.

PAULA! WITH A SMILE NOW . . .

I SHOULD HAVE GONE TO ACTING SCHOOL.

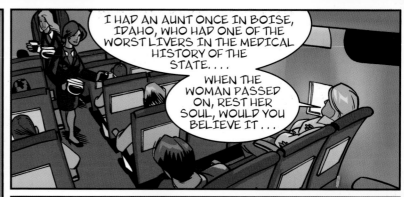

I HAD AN AUNT ONCE IN BOISE, IDAHO, WHO HAD ONE OF THE WORST LIVERS IN THE MEDICAL HISTORY OF THE STATE. . . .

WHEN THE WOMAN PASSED ON, REST HER SOUL, WOULD YOU BELIEVE IT . . .

. . . THERE WERE FIVE MEDICAL ASSOCIATIONS BIDDING JUST TO GET HER LIVER IN A BOTTLE ON DISPLAY.

OH DEAR . . . I AM SO SORRY!

FORGET IT.

IMAGINE THAT, ALL THEM DOCTORS WANTING A BAD LIVER.

WHAT'D YOU SAY?

HUH?

WHAT KIND OF WORK DO YOU DO?

DISCHARGED FROM THE AIR FORCE.

UH-HUH . . .

SORRY, JANIE!

ISN'T THAT WONDERFUL! BROTHER OF MINE WAS IN THE NAVY DURING THE WAR. HE WAS ON AN AIRCRAFT CARRIER—OR WAS IT A BATTLESHIP?

DID YOU FEEL ANYTHING A MOMENT AGO... SENSATION OF SPEED? ACCELERATION?

WELL, I FELT A LITTLE QUEASY WHEN WE TOOK OFF, BUT MY LATE HUSBAND USED TO SAY... COULD YOU HAND ME A PILLOW PLEASE...

ALL RIGHT...

FINE...

PROPERTY OF DAWSON PINKNEY

HE USED TO SAY THAT I HAD A STOMACH LIKE A...

...NEWBORN BABY...

CAN'T KEEP NOTHING DOWN.

GOT A LITTLE NERVES, MISS?

SORRY.

SIT STILL AND ENJOY YOUR FLIGHT, OR I'LL HAVE YOU ARRESTED IN NEW YORK FOR ASSAULTING A FLIGHT ATTENDANT. OKAY?

boing boing

I GUESS WE'RE EVEN NOW?

I'LL TAKE IT FROM HERE, SIR.

THANKS AND ALL THAT. TAKE YOUR SEAT.

THAT WAS REAL . . . NICE OF YOU, YOUNG MAN.

WHO IS THAT GUY?

CERTIFIABLE NUT JOB, THAT'S WHO. FIRST HE WANTS HERBAL TEA, THEN CASHEWS—NOW HE THINKS THE WORLD'S ENDING! SEE WHY YOU GOTTA STAY CALM?

STILL ACCELERATING, SKIPPER.

MAYBE WE CAN FIND A LITTLE MORE AIR AND SLOW THIS CRATE DOWN.

JFK, JFK, TRANS-OCEAN 3-3 REQUESTING ALTITUDE CHANGE TO FLIGHT LEVEL TWO-FIVE-ZERO, ACKNOWLEDGE...

IT'S POINTLESS, CAPTAIN. EITHER THEY'RE OFF WHACK... EVERYBODY OUT THERE...

OR **WE** ARE.

WYATT, TRY TO NOTIFY JFK WE'RE GOING TO TWENTY-FIVE THOUSAND. MAYBE THEY CAN HEAR US.

MAGELLAN, CALL IT OUT— LET ME KNOW WHAT'S GOING ON.

WE SHOULD SAY SOMETHING TO THE PASSENGERS ABOUT THIS, SKIPPER.

CRAIG, TELL THE PASSENGERS WE'VE DESCENDED TO TWENTY-FIVE THOUSAND...

...TO LOOK FOR SOME SMOOTHER AIR.

WHAT WAS THAT?!!

!?!

BOY, WHEN THEY SAID FASTEN YOUR SEAT BELTS, THEY WEREN'T KIDDING! I DON'T THINK I'VE EVER BEEN ON A PLANE THIS BUMPY BEFORE!!

WHAT YOU TRYING TO SEE OUT THERE?

YEEHAW!

I JUST LOVE THAT FEELING OF DROPPING. YOU GOTTA LOVE IT.

AIN'T NOTHING BUT A LITTLE AIR POCKET.

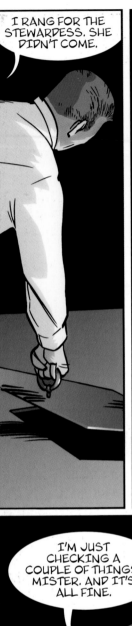

I RANG FOR THE STEWARDESS. SHE DIDN'T COME.

UM, SIR, IF YOU WOULD JUST GO BACK TO YOUR SEAT . . . EVERYTHING IS UNDER CONTROL.

TELL IT TO THE SHEEP. I WANT THE TRUTH. THERE WAS A WHITE FLASH!

DON'T GIVE ME THAT ATMOSPHERIC TURBULENCE BALONEY. I KNOW A THING OR TWO. I'VE FLOWN MISSIONS OVER ENEMY TERRITORY.

WHAT KIND OF TROUBLE ARE WE IN?

I'M JUST CHECKING A COUPLE OF THINGS, MISTER. AND IT'S ALL FINE.

HOW'S ABOUT I GO BACK TO THE COCKPIT AND YOU GO BACK TO YOUR SEAT?

UNLESS YOU'D RATHER GET OUT AND WALK . . .

I THINK I MET YOUR HERBAL TEA NUTCASE GUY.

I CAN HANDLE HIM.

IF YOU CAN'T, LET US KNOW, OKAY . . . ?

COPACETIC BACK THERE, EXCEPT FOR THE CRAZY PEOPLE.

GOOD. . . . WHAT'S OUR SPEED NOW?

THE LORAN'S OUT.

OUT?

THAT'S AFFIRMATIVE, IT'S OUT.

CRAIG, WHAT'S OUR FUEL?

29,435 POUNDS.

I DON'T FEEL THE ACCELERATION ANYMORE.

MAGELLAN, HOW ABOUT THAT HEADING TO JFK?

THIS IS PART SCIENTIFIC, SKIPPER... PART KENTUCKY WINDAGE. TRY TWO-SIX-TWO... CLOSE AS I CAN MAKE IT.

SMOOTHER NOW...

ALL RIGHT, GENTLEMEN, YOU KNOW WHAT WE'RE UP AGAINST.

NO RADIO, NO GROUND RADAR POINTS, NO SPECIFICS ON WHERE WE ARE. AND THIS BEAST IS GULPING FUEL...

WE'VE GOT ONE CHANCE—GO DOWN THROUGH THIS OVERCAST AND LOOK FOR SOMETHING FAMILIAR. KEEP A SHARP LOOKOUT FOR OTHER TRAFFIC... AND KEEP YOUR FINGERS CROSSED.

A FEW PRAYERS WOULDN'T BE OUT OF ORDER, EITHER.

SEAT BELT

bing bing

I LEFT MINE ON FROM LAST TIME. THEY SURE HAVE YOU PUTTING THEM ON AND TAKING THEM OFF.

BANKING AND DESCENDING? IT'S NOT TIME FOR FINAL APPROACH.

I SEEN A PLANE ON TV ONCE, SMALL PLANE MIND YOU, LANDING GEAR WOULDN'T COME DOWN.

THEY MADE IT.

SOMEBODY DROVE ALONG UNDERNEATH AND PULLED IT DOWN BY HAND FROM A PICKUP TRUCK . . .

I DON'T SEE WHY THEY CAN'T DIG A BIG TUNNEL UNDER THE ATLANTIC. THEN YOU COULD JUST DRIVE TO LONDON . . .

THEY DON'T TELL YOU ABOUT THE HYDRAULIC OIL THAT'S SPEWING OUT OR THE BOLTS THEY FORGOT TO TIGHTEN, BECAUSE THEY'RE AFRAID YOU'LL GO CRAZY.

WELL, NOW, I DON'T KNOW THAT I'D GO JUMPING TO—

I'M NOT JUST GOING TO STAY PUT ANYMORE!

click

THIS WASN'T MY FAULT! I'M GONNA TELL THEM. THEY'RE GONNA KNOW!

HERE HE COMES...

WHO?

HIM! 27D—THE TROUBLEMAKER!

I DEMAND TO SEE THE PILOT, RIGHT NOW!

SSSSSSSSSSS

HAAAAEEEEEEEEEEEE!!

GRAB HIM!

STAND ASIDE, LADIES.

UNNN . . .

NICE WORK!

I SEEN HIM RUSHING UP HERE. I KNEW SOMETHING WAS BOTHERING HIM.

HAVE YOU ALL GONE NUTS?!

LET ME UP. WE'RE GONNA DIE ON THIS CRATE!

HE'S GOING TO SCARE THE PASSENGERS TO DEATH!

WHY DON'T YA JUST CALM DOWN AND TRY TO ACT A LITTLE NICER, MISTER?!

THE PLANE IS—

MMMPH!

DON'T YOU WORRY, MA'AM. HE AIN'T GONNA DO NO MORE HOLLERING.

I HATE TO BE A BOTHER, BUT WE HAVE A SITUATION . . .

PAST FIVE THOUSAND, SKIPPER . . .

WE'RE GOING TO BE SMACK DAB IN THE MIDDLE OF TWENTY OTHER FLIGHTS!

YOU GOT ANOTHER ALTERNATIVE, CRAIG? WE GOTTA FIND LANDMARKS OR GO VFR.

LOOK! I'D CALL THAT A LANDMARK.

click!

LADIES AND GENTLEMEN, WE HOPE YOU'RE ENJOYING YOUR FLIGHT. PLEASE CONTINUE TO OBSERVE THE FASTEN SEAT BELT SIGNS.

THANK GOD WE'LL BE ON THE GROUND SOON.

SEE, THE LIGHT AND THE NOISE YOU WERE SO WORRIED ABOUT— NOTHING.

WE'LL BE ON THE GROUND ANY MINUTE.

SAY, IF I LET GO, YOU GONNA BEHAVE YOURSELF?

WE SHOULD BE LANDING IN NEW YORK SHORTLY. THANK YOU FOR FLYING TRANS-OCEAN.

click!

I DON'T KNOW IF THAT'S A GOOD IDEA.

AW, HE AIN'T GONNA DO NOTHING . . .

. . . ARE YOU?

SPLUT . . . BANG AND A BRIGHT LIGHT ONCE ON A C-130 I'S ON. ENGINE BLEW UP. WENT DOWN.

I—I BAILED OUT BY MYSELF. EVERYBODY DIED.

SPENT A WEEK ON THIS MOUNTAINTOP—COLD. ENEMY LOOKING FOR ME EVERYWHERE . . .

THEN, AFTER . . . THEY SAID IT WAS A MAINTENANCE ISSUE— MY FAULT, SEE?

I WANTED TO TALK TO THE PILOT. I JUST WANTED TO TELL HIM THAT IT WASN'T MY FAULT . . .

I THINK IT'S ALL BLOWN OVER. HE WASN'T GONNA DO NOTHING NOHOW.

ALL RIGHT, I GUESS . . . JUST KEEP HIM QUIET.

SHOULD WE JUST LEAVE THEM THERE LIKE THAT?

WE DON'T HAVE A CHOICE. IT'S JUST YOU AND ME. WE'VE GOT TO GET READY FOR LANDING.

HEY, DON'T FORGET... RIDE OF THE VALKYRIES. YOU MIGHT JUST MAKE IT AFTER ALL.

SIR, BE SURE YOUR TRAY IS UP AND YOUR SEAT IS ALL THE WAY FORWARD, PLEASE.

UH... OKAY...

PLEASE PUT YOUR SEAT IN THE UPRIGHT POSITION FOR LANDING, MA'AM.

FEELING BETTER?

I'LL FEEL BETTER WHEN MY FEET ARE ON THE GROUND AGAIN.

YOU BAILED OUT, HUH?

SOME BOLT LIKELY GOT LOOSE, WENT INTO THE TURBO—A BANG, WHITE FLASH, A LOT OF FIRE.

THEN EVERYBODY WAS DEAD—EXCEPT ME. I FOUND A CHUTE.

THE ENEMY SAW MY CHUTE AND THEY WANTED TO DRAG MY CARCASS THROUGH THE VILLAGES.

IT'S GOT TO BE SOMEBODY'S FAULT. UNDERSTAND?

UH-HUH... CAN'T SAY AS I KNOW WHAT YOU'RE GETTING AT, MISTER.

HOW ABOUT JFK?

NOTHING DOING. VHF IS OUT.

TRY HIGH FREQUENCY.

I DID ALREADY, SKIPPER. NOTHING.

TRY LAGUARDIA. KEEP USING HIGH FREQUENCY.

LAGUARDIA, THIS IS TRANS-OCEAN 3-3. LAGUARDIA, TRANS-OCEAN 3-3.

THIS IS LAGUARDIA TOWER. WHO IS CALLING PLEASE?

THANK GOD.

THIS IS TRANS-OCEAN 3-3, LAGUARDIA. WE'RE ON THE NORTHEAST LEG OF THE LAGUARDIA RANGE.

REQUEST RADAR VECTOR TO JFK ILS. WE ALSO HAVE A PASSENGER OF CONCERN AND REQUEST SECURITY STANDING BY.

A RADAR VECTOR— TO JFK.

WHAT ARE YOU, A WISE GUY? YOU'D LIKE WHAT? TO WHERE? WHAT KIND OF SECURITY YOU TALKING ABOUT?

WHAT FLIGHT DID YOU SAY THIS WAS?

COME ON, LAGUARDIA, QUIT FOOLING AROUND. WE'RE LOW ON FUEL.

WHAT KIND OF AIRCRAFT IS THIS?

THIS IS TRANS-OCEAN 3-3. A BOEING 7-0-7 AND WE—

DID YOU SAY A BOEING 2-4-7?

THEY'LL BE WAITING FOR ME IN NEW YORK, PUT ME AWAY FOR GOOD.

YOU THINK I'M A CRAZY PERSON, HUH?

IT CROSSED MY MIND ONCE OR TWICE.

NOW, I'M NOT SO SURE WHO'S CRAZY . . .

LET'S GO BACK AND SIT WHERE WE BELONG.

'CAUSE, MISTER, IT SOUNDS LIKE YOU HAD IT ROUGH. BUT WE'RE ALL ON THIS BIRD TOGETHER AND NOBODY'S LANDING UNTIL WE ALL DO.

WHAT DO WE DO ABOUT IT, SKIPPER?

I SAY WE REV THIS BABY UP AND CLIMB UNTIL WE HIT THAT JET STREAM AGAIN, AND TRY TO GET BACK TO WHERE WE BELONG.

ALL RIGHT, CRAIG . . . LET'S DO IT!

IT WAS JUST A SPELL HE WAS HAVING. HE'S FINE.

WELL, I'M NOT FINE! I THOUGHT WE WAS FIXING TO LAND. WHY WE GOING BACK UP?

IF HE GETS UP AGAIN, I'M GOING TO GET THE CAPTAIN. UNDERSTAND?

YES, MA'AM.

HATCH, GET ME A HEADING FOR NEW YORK. CRAIG, WHAT'S OUR FUEL LOOK LIKE?

SKIPPER . . . HA HA HA . . . UNBELIEVABLE . . . HA HA HA . . .

THE FUEL . . . IT'S BACK TO 29,435 POUNDS. HA HA . . . CAN YOU BEAT THAT?

BUTTON IT UP! STAY SHARP. AT LEAST WE WON'T HAVE TO DITCH IN THE OCEAN.

UM . . . GENTLEMEN, WHAT AM I SUPPOSED TO TELL THE PASSENGERS?

WE WILL FIGURE THIS OUT . . . JUST TRY TO KEEP THEM CALM UNTIL WE DO.

CALM? THANKS A LOT . . . I'VE GOT ONE NUTCASE ATTACKING THE COCKPIT, AND THE REST OF THEM AREN'T TOO FAR BEHIND! SURE, I'LL JUST KEEP THEM CALM!

WE SHOULD BE APPROACHING NEW YORK NOW, SKIPPER.

THIS IS THE EXACT SPOT WHERE WE TURNED AWAY FROM LAGUARDIA—LONGITUDE, LATITUDE, MINUTE, SECOND!

SO WHERE IS IT?

IT SHOULD BE RIGHT THERE! UNLESS MY COMPASS HAS GONE NUTS TOO, WE'RE DEAD ON IT, SKIPPER!

I DON'T THINK YOUR COMPASS IS OFF, HATCH.

WHAT?

IT'S ALL UNDERWATER.

SKIPPER, HAVE YOU FLIPPED? UNDERWATER?

NEW YORK WAS COVERED BY A SHALLOW SEA DURING MOST OF THE CRETACEOUS PERIOD. TIME OF THE GREAT DINOSAURS—T. REX . . . PALEONTOLOGY IS A HOBBY OF MINE.

SO MAYBE WE SLIPPED TOO FAR AND IN THE WRONG DIRECTION . . . MAYBE THE COMPASS IS OFF.

LET'S FIND SOME LAND, BE SURE OF OUR BEARINGS.

WHEN WE LAND, I'LL BUY YOU ALL A DRINK SOMEPLACE—HOW'S THAT?

I DON'T DRINK. YOU DO WHAT YOU WANT.

YEAH, THAT'LL BE REAL NICE . . . REAL NICE . . .

GOOD.

I'D SAY WE'RE AT ABOUT THREE THOUSAND FEET.

WANT ANOTHER PILLOW? I THINK THERE'S ONE UP IN THE—

AIN'T NOTHING BUT A BIG SHINY MIRROR OUT THERE . . .

MIRROR?? YOU MEAN THE OCEAN? WE WERE ON FINAL APPROACH!

WHAT HAPPENED TO MANHATTAN? WE WERE GOING TO LAND . . .

MAYBE WE'RE CIRCLING AROUND AND CAN'T SEE IT. YOU GONNA GET THAT PILLOW?

THAT DOESN'T MAKE ANY SENSE . . .

HAND CREAM

THERE'S LAND! HAPPY NOW? THE SOONER WE GET HOME THE BETTER.

I'LL GET THAT PILLOW FOR YOU NOW.

NOW YOU KEEP THAT SEAT BELT FASTENED, OKAY?

AREN'T YOU THOUGHTFUL . . .

PROPERTY OF DAWSON PINKNEY

JANIE, WHAT'S GOING ON IN THERE? WHAT'S ALL THIS UP AND DOWN NONSENSE? PEOPLE ARE GOING TO BE RIOTING SOON. WHY CAN'T THOSE FLY PEOPLE DO SOMETHING?

LISTEN, BACK HERE IT'S UP TO US!

WE'LL KEEP ORDER IF WE HAVE TO PERSONALLY SIT ON THEM ALL. WE'LL START WITH THAT ONE NUTCASE. COME ON, PAULA!

WHERE'D HE GO?

HE'LL BE RIGHT BACK, I EXPECT.

OH NO!

ARE YOU ALL RIGHT?

UGH . . . WHAT HAPPENED?

MY STARS! ARE THOSE CATTLE ON THE BEACH THERE?

WHAT IS THAT?

THAT LOOKS LIKE THE BAHAMAS.

WHERE ARE WE?

WHERE'S THE AIRPORT?

EVERYONE, STAY CALM.

I'M CHECKING OUT. NO WAY I'M GOING TO SIT AROUND AND WAIT TO BE ARRESTED WHEN WE GET TO NEW YORK. I HAVEN'T DONE ANYTHING WRONG. NONE OF THIS IS MY FAULT!

WHAT DO YOU THINK YOU'RE DOING?

FWP

WHAT JUST HAPPENED?!

WE'VE DECOMPRESSED—EMERGENCY PROCEDURES!

COME ON! LET'S MAKE SURE THE REST OF THE PASSENGERS DON'T JUMP OUT.

CRAIG, ALTITUDE?

STEADY AT TWENTY-FIVE HUNDRED! WE'RE ALL RIGHT.

WYATT! GET BACK THERE FAST. FIND OUT WHAT'S GOING ON.

I'M ON MY WAY!

EVERYONE, STAY IN YOUR SEAT. KEEP YOUR SEAT BELT FASTENED!

JANIE, WHAT HAPPENED?

THAT CRAZY GUY—HE OPENED THE DOOR AND JUMPED OUT THE BACK OF THE PLANE. ALL THE OXYGEN MASKS DROPPED DOWN AUTOMATICALLY.

WE GOT TO GET THAT DOOR CLOSED.

PAULA, HONEY, DO WHAT YOU CAN. I'LL BE RIGHT BACK TO HELP.

AND NOW SEARCHED FOR ON LAND, SEA, AND AIR BY ANGUISHED HUMAN BEINGS FEARFUL OF WHAT THEY'LL FIND.

BUT YOU AND I KNOW WHAT'S HAPPENED . . .

SO, IF SOME MOMENT . . . ANY MOMENT . . . YOU HEAR THE SOUND OF JET ENGINES . . .

. . . FLYING ATOP THE OVERCAST, ENGINES THAT SOUND SEARCHING AND LOST, ENGINES THAT SOUND DESPERATE . . .

. . . SHOOT UP A FLARE OR DO SOMETHING . . . THAT WOULD BE TRANS-OCEAN 33, TRYING TO GET HOME . . . FROM THE TWILIGHT ZONE.

The Odyssey of Flight 33

Season Two, Episode #18

Original Air Date: February 24, 1961

Written by Rod Serling

Cast

Narrator: Rod Serling

Captain Farver: John Anderson*
*Also appeared in *A Passage for Trumpet* as Gabriel
Of Late I Think of Cliffordville as Diedrich
The Old Man in the Cave as Goldsmith

First Officer Craig: Paul Comi*
*Also appeared in *People Are Alike All Over* as Mark Marcusson
The Parallel as Psychiatrist

Navigator Hatch: Sandy Kenyon*
*Also appeared in *The Shelter* as Frank Henderson
Valley of the Shadow as Gas Station Attendant

Second Officer Wyatt: Wayne Heffley*
*Also appeared in *Black Leather Jackets* as Mover (uncredited)

Flight Engineer Purcell: Harp McGuire

Janie: Beverly Brown

Paula: Nancy Rennick*
*Also appeared in *The After Hours* as Miss Keevers

Passenger: Betty Garde*
*Also appeared in *The Midnight Sun* as Mrs. Bronson

Passenger: Jay Overholts*
*Also appeared in *Where Is Everybody?* as Reporter #2 (as Jay Overholt)
One for the Angels as Doctor
A Thing About Machines as Intern
Twenty Two as Actor (uncredited)
Static as Man #2 (uncredited)
The Jungle as Taxi Driver (as Jay Overholt)
Showdown with Rance McGrew as Cowboy #2

RAF Man: Lester Fletcher

Crew

Producer: Buck Houghton

Director: Justus Addiss

Director of Photography: George T. Clemens

Film Editor: Bill Mosher

Technical Advisor/Aviation Editor: Robert J. Serling

Special Effects/Dinosaur Sequence: Jack H. Harris

Production Notes

The dinosaur sequence in *The Odyssey of Flight 33*, which cost $2,500, was the most expensive special effect ever used in any episode of *The Twilight Zone*. It was filmed using stop-motion animation and puppets that were originally created for the movie *Dinosaurus!*

The cockpit dialogue is remarkably accurate due to advice from Rod Serling's brother, Robert, who was an aviation writer for United Press International. Robert met with a pilot for TWA and together they came up with many of the lines for the flight crew.

ADAPTING STORIES FROM ROD SERLING'S
THE TWILIGHT ZONE

In terms of screenwriting adaptations it's trying to cut out stuff that's extraneous, without doing damage to the original piece, because you owe a debt of some respect to the original author.

—Rod Serling, 1975

At first, the idea sounded straightforward. Take an original *Twilight Zone* screenplay and adapt it into a graphic novel—break the visuals into panels, move the dialogue into balloons and captions. After all, Rod Serling himself was a fan of comics, and graphic novels are their visual and literary heirs. Serling collected Entertaining Comics titles such as *Tales from the Crypt* and *Weird Science*, the themes of which resonate in *The Twilight Zone*; even Serling's trademark narration could be considered an echo of the Crypt Keeper's introductions. Yet the more I considered the task of adapting the scripts, the more the gravity of what I was doing set in. I grew up watching *The Twilight Zone*, after all, as did so many Americans. The work required a certain reverential perspective, considering the show's iconic status, not to mention the quality of the original material.

In the 1950s the comics Serling had enjoyed were considered subversive, a threat to America's youth. Frederick Wertham published *Seduction of the Innocent* in 1954, excoriating comics in an atmosphere of public paranoia similar to a scene from *The Monsters Are Due on Maple Street*. A year later, a Senate committee was convened to investigate the pernicious influence of horror comics on America's youth, and the Comics Code Authority was established to censor comics' content. EC Comics went out of business as a direct result. In an interesting twist of fate, by the end of the decade *The Twilight Zone* was just beginning to find its television audience with stories that probably would not have made it past the comics censors. Recreating Serling's stories now, in graphic novel form, seems appropriate, emblematic of an era in which comics are finding a new readership, achieving new respect, and speaking to a new audience receptive to a more sophisticated message.

Serling's stories run the gamut from serious drama, filled with fantastic and frightening dilemmas of the human condition, to wry, tongue-in-cheek humor in a sci-fi wrapper. Selecting eight as graphic novel material meant making difficult choices. Serling was a prolific writer, creating more than half of *The Twilight Zone's* 156 scripts. It was not only a question of which of these would work best in novelized format, but which ones, as a group, would come closest to capturing the essence of *The Twilight Zone*. The stories ultimately chosen for these books possess the strongest visual possibilities and reflect an effort to achieve a cross section of Serling's dramatic range.

As I began adapting the stories for artists, I immersed myself in the screenplays and watched each episode until I felt I had internalized not just the characters, the plot, and the point, but what I imagined to be something of the author himself. In the process, I felt a growing kinship with Serling. Parts of the screenplay were often deleted from the actual show. Lines, characters, even entire scenes were struck, sometimes for budgetary reasons, sometimes because of time constraints, sometimes perhaps because Serling himself may have anticipated problems with the scenes. The show usually had only a thirty-minute time slot. The deleted scenes, however, often add richness and complexity to the story, offering a glimmer into what Serling might have done were it not for the constraints of the television medium. Restoring scenes seemed to help push the story even harder. I felt as if I were developing Serling's original design, following the telling to its logical conclusion.

With each of these stories, I have aspired to take advantage of what the graphic novel format can do. Art and text draw the reader deeply into the narrative. The reader does not just hear, but ponders, actively bridging the gaps between the panels of art with his or her own imagination. The story doesn't just happen to the reader, but, in part, *is* the reader. In other words, *The Twilight Zone* episodes had to be recreated not just to fit into a graphic novel format but to belong to it.

As much as possible, I have endeavored to keep the intentions of the original story intact—that is the "debt of respect" owed to Serling—fully functional in a new medium. From some nearby fifth dimension, I hope Serling is smiling at the prospect of these books, pleased at the thought of a new generation arriving by way of a different avenue perhaps, but entering and being welcomed into the fold of "Zonies" around the world.

—Mark Kneece
Professor of Sequential Art, Savannah College of Art and Design

Acknowledgments

Our thanks go to Carol Serling for her time and consideration while reviewing the adaptation texts and illustrated pages, and also to John Lowe, chair of the Sequential Art Department at Savannah College of Art and Design, for his assistance in pairing the right artists with the right stories.

Bloomsbury Publishing, London, Berlin and New York

First published in Great Britain in 2009 by Bloomsbury Publishing Plc
36 Soho Square, London, W1D 3QY

First published in the USA in 2009 by Walker & Company
175 Fifth Avenue, New York, NY 10010

Packaged by Design Press, a division of Savannah College of Art and Design, Inc.*
22 East Lathrop Street, Savannah, Georgia 31415, USA

Adaptation from Rod Serling's original script by Mark Kneece
Illustrated by Robert Grabe
Coloring by Caravan Studio
Lettering by Thomas Zielonka
Series title treatment by Devin O'Bryan
Series copyediting by Kerri O'Hern
Series creative development by Anna Marlis Burgard and Emily Easton
Series art direction and design by Angela Rojas
Series project management by Angela Rojas and Melissa Kavonic
Creative consultant: Carol Serling

Photograph of Rod Serling © Bettmann/Corbis

A CIP catalogue record of this book is available from the British Library

ISBN 978 0 7475 8788 0

Printed in China by C & C Offset

1 3 5 7 9 10 8 6 4 2

All papers used by Bloomsbury Publishing are natural, recyclable products made from wood grown in well-managed forests. The manufacturing processes conform to the environmental regulations of the country of origin

www.bloomsbury.com/childrens
The Savannah College of Art and Design: www.scad.edu